Hans Christian Andersen
Children's Favorite Stories

Hans Christian Andersen
Children's Favorite Stories

Retold by Lornie Leete-Hodge

Illustrated by Ronald Embleton

Originally published in England by Dean & Sons, Ltd.
Published in United States and simultaneously in Canada by Joshua Morris, Inc.
431 Post Road East
Westport, CT 06880
Copyright © The Hamlyn Publishing Group, Ltd. 1983
All Rights Reserved

ISBN 0-887-05056-5

Made and printed in Great Britain by
Purnell and Sons (Book Production) Ltd.,
Member of the BPCC Group, Paulton, Bristol

Contents

The Emperor's New Clothes

Many years ago, there was an Emperor who was fat and rich and very proud. All he cared about was clothes.

"What shall I wear today?" he would ask. He could never make up his mind. He had so many clothes in the cupboards they spilled out into the room. There were clothes everywhere! He had a special room just for his clothes, and soon it was not nearly big enough. He would put on a new suit for every hour of the day. If he went out into the streets, he put on *special* finery. He wanted the whole world to admire him. All day long he would preen in front of the mirror. If anyone wanted to see him, there he was looking in the mirror! Can you imagine such a vain man?

One day, two strangers came to the city. It was not long before they heard of the Emperor and his love of clothes. They were cunning and made a plan. They would get rich because of this silly Emperor. They went to visit him at the Palace.

"Your Majesty," they said, bowing low. "You are the most magnificent king we have ever seen, and we have travelled far and wide. Oh, there is no finer king in all the world, except . . ." They stopped and looked at each other.

"Tell me, who is finer than I am? Tell me!" cried the king.

"Oh, a king in a far off land," they replied. "But if we made you a special suit, you would be the finest in the whole world. We would make you a suit so rare, so fine, that none could equal it. You see, we would make you a very special suit."

And they bowed low and smiled at each other. They knew the king could not resist their offer. Their fortunes would soon be made. Oh, it was so easy!

The Emperor was pleased. "But I have the finest clothes in the world," he said. "Isn't this the best suit you have ever seen?" And he turned this way and that before the mirror, showing himself off.

"Oh yes, yours *is* a magnificent suit, Your Majesty," they told him. "But if we made you a suit, it would be the best suit ever made. We would make you a *magic* suit!"

The Emperor wanted to know more. "A magic suit?" the Emperor spluttered. "But, how, what?"

"It will be the most beautiful suit you have ever seen," said the two men who were posing as weavers.

"But how is it magic?" interrupted the Emperor.

"Ah, that is the secret," they told him. "Leave it to us!"

"But I must know," the Emperor stamped his foot.

"It's like this," they replied. "Our suit can be seen only by those who are clever and wise and well suited to their work. Those who are dull and stupid cannot see anything. The suit would be invisible to them."

"Invisible!" cried the Emperor. "Oh, I like that!" And he rubbed his hands.

"Oh, quite invisible," said the weavers, rubbing theirs.

The Emperor walked up and down. "This is perfect," he murmured to himself. "I will have a wonderful new suit which will tell me who is clever and who is stupid. And I will look marvellous at the same time. Oh, what could be better!"

"It will be *very* expensive," warned the weavers. "We shall need a thousand gold crowns to buy the material!"

The Emperor did not care. He *must* have that suit. So he gave the weavers the golden crowns and told them to make his suit.

"Hurry, hurry, hurry," he told them for he could not bear to wait.

The weavers were given a special room in the palace with a fine loom. They had rolls of silks of all colours, and reels and reels of gold thread—everything they asked for was given them. They worked far into the night. The click-clack of the loom could be heard, but the door was fast shut. No one must see their work until it was finished.

The Emperor was beside himself with excitement. "I must see for myself," he said. He could hardly wait for his suit!

"Your Majesty, is that wise?" asked one of his ministers. "Remember what they told you."

"Oh, very well," said the Emperor, in a sulky way. "Then you must go. Go and look at my suit and tell me about it. Go on. *Now*!"

So the minister went to see the weavers. They were very busy. The loom was moving up and down and along and across. But there was no cloth! He rubbed his eyes. This was very strange. He looked again. The loom was empty!

"Good morning, Sir," said the weavers. "Isn't this cloth the best you have ever seen in your whole life?"

"Oh yes, yes, the cloth is perfect," said the minister. He must not let them know he could not see anything. He must pretend to see the cloth and everyone would know how wise he was, and the best minister the king had ever had.

"Do you like the colour?" asked the weavers, holding up their arms as if to show the cloth.

"Indeed I do. It is just perfect! What brightness, what richness! Oh! I wish I could have a suit like it myself! The king will love it."

"We knew you would like it," smiled the weavers," for you are the wisest man in the kingdom. Please tell the Emperor all about it. And we shall need more thread and pearls for the trimming."

"Anything, anything," promised the minister. And off he went to order the pearls and thread and report to the Emperor.

"Well, what is it like?" asked the Emperor biting his nails in his excitement. "Is it truly magnificent?"

"Oh yes, Your Majesty," said the minister, "I have never seen anything to compare with it."

But the Emperor still wondered and worried. Oh why were they taking so long? He wanted his suit now! He sent two of his favourite courtiers to look at the work. They came back and said the same as the minister. The suit was the best in the world. He could contain himself no longer. He *had* to see for himself!

"Your Majesty," said the weavers, bowing to the ground, "this is an honour. Your suit is nearly finished. Isn't it beautiful? Almost too beautiful to wear!"

The Emperor looked at them and looked away. He stared again. But there was nothing. There was no cloth on the loom and no cloth on the arm of the weaver who stood there smiling and bowing. But if he said so, they would think he was a fool. So he clapped his hands in delight.

"Oh, it's lovely. I shall be the talk of the town, the country—the whole world!" he cried. "You shall be the Lord High Weavers," he said and ordered that a medal be made for them.

"Your Majesty is too kind," smirked the weavers.

"We shall have a Grand Procession," said the Emperor. "Everyone must see my suit. Tell the crier to go into the streets. The people will look out for me. Oh, isn't this the most exciting day!"

So it was all arranged. The bands would play, the Emperor would walk through the streets, the crowds would turn out to see him. Above his head, four courtiers would hold a silk canopy.

At long, long last the weavers said the suit was ready. They could do no more.

The whole court watched as the weavers bowed low before the Emperor. He stood waiting for them to help him put on the suit.

"First of all, the silk shirt," they said. "Isn't it the softest you have ever worn?"

"It's very soft," agreed the Emperor, moving his arms as if to feel the softness.

"Now, the breeches," they crooned steadying him as he put one leg, then the other, into the air. "Slip them on, just a little higher! There! That's right."

And they tweaked the fastenings round his waist. The Emperor turned and twirled but still could not see anything! He had had mirrors put all round his room to see his special suit, but all he saw was himself. No suit!

"Here is the coat! See how it hangs, just the right trimming, don't you think?"

Once again the Emperor lifted his arms and the weavers pulled and straightened. He could not even *feel* it, let alone see it! But all the court was clapping and cheering. He must look marvellous!

"Here is the cloak!" the weavers cried. "Look at the velvet, how it shines in the sunlight! Purple for a king, and perfect with the coat. There! Just one more clasp and you are ready." The weavers bowed.

The Emperor picked up his crown and settled it on his head. *That* he could feel and see, but everyone was still clapping. "Hoorah!" they cried, "what an Emperor! He is the finest man in the whole world.

"How do I look?" asked the Emperor, for he could see nothing but his crown.

"Oh, perfect, Your Majesty!" cried the courtiers. "No one has ever seen you look so fine."

Four of them took up the silk canopy and held it high above his head. The bands played, and the people lining the streets cheered and waved. The Emperor stepped out, smiling and preening.

"Hurrah for the Emperor!" they all shouted.

"What a suit," cried some, and pointed. "What style, what colours!"

13

The noise was deafening. And the Emperor walked on smiling and happy. He had never felt so proud in his whole life.

No one would admit he was a fool, so all cheered and clapped and waved until their throats were dry, their hands sore and their arms ached. The Emperor knew it was the most perfect day of his whole life. The weavers were right, it was a *magic* suit.

Then, suddenly, a small boy in the crowd looked at the Emperor and cried out in the sudden quiet, "But he's got nothing on!"

"Ssh, what are you saying?" said his father.

"But he's got nothing on, I tell you!" said the boy. "HE'S GOT NOTHING ON!"

Soon, the crowd took up the cry and everyone laughed and jeered.

The Emperor knew they were right. But he drew up his head, he walked tall and straight, waving and smiling as if nothing had happened. The bands played and the people cheered once more. Everyone enjoyed the joke.

But as for the weavers, no one has ever heard of them again!

The Real Princess

Long ago in a far away land, there lived a Prince. One day, he decided it was time to marry, so he set off in search of a real princess. Of course, he could not think of marrying anyone else.

He travelled far and wide, and met many princesses. Some were tall, some short, some very young and some even old. He liked one with fair hair, but her feet were too big! He liked another with dark hair, but wished her eyes were blue. He was very fussy. None pleased him.

He came home feeling very sad.

"Oh, Mother," he said to the Queen, "I have searched everywhere. I cannot find a real princess to marry. What shall I do?"

"Never mind," said the Queen, who was a wise woman. "One day, a real princess will come along. Wait and see!"

He waited and fretted and stared out of the window. The road was empty. There was no real princess in sight.

That night it rained. The thunder roared and the lightning flashed. There had never been such a storm. All at once, there was a loud knocking on the Palace door.

"Who can be out in this weather?" wondered the Queen.

A Princess stood on the doorstep. But no one knew who she was. She was wet and cold, with windblown hair which hung damp on her head, and her clothes were bedraggled.

"I am a *real* Princess," she said, "may I come in?"

"We shall soon find out," muttered the Queen to herself. She took the Princess to warm by the fire. Then she went to make ready.

The finest room was prepared. The Queen made the servants remove all the bedding. Then, from the store cupboard, she took one very small, very hard, dried pea and put it carefully under the

mattress. The servants piled first one, then another, mattress on top, twenty in all. But she was not satisfied.

"Put these feather beds on as well," she ordered. So the servants, struggling and heaving, put twenty feather mattresses on top. At last it was ready. The Princess climbed up a ladder and lay down. She had never slept in so high a bed!

Next morning the Princess was pale and tired. "Did you sleep well?" asked the Queen.

"No, I hardly slept at all," said the Princess. "There was something in my bed. Something hard and horrid, no matter which way I turned, I felt it. I am black and blue."

At once the Queen knew she *must* be a real Princess. No one else would have noticed one little pea under all those mattresses. So the Prince asked her to marry him and they lived happily ever after.

As for the pea, it was put in a museum for everyone to see.

The Ugly Duckling

It was a warm, sunny day. Bees and butterflies danced in the garden, and the scent of flowers was all around. By the pond, the large white duck stretched herself on her nest. She had been sitting on her eggs for such a long time. Would they ever hatch? she wondered.

In the field, the cows stood in silence munching the lush grass. The old donkey was by the fence. He was always there, watching. The hens in the yard, scratched about in the dust, clacking to themselves. Old Tom, the farm cat, was fast asleep on the cobbles by the barn door. He moved in his sleep and purred. He loved the sun.

The pond was busy with ducks swimming and diving. None of them bothered about their friend on the nest, they were too happy catching fish and insects. She longed to join them. "Quack!" she called, but they went on swimming. She sighed. "Come on ducklings, hurry up and hatch!" she said.

As if they had heard her, the tiny, fluffy ducklings began to crack their shells. Slowly, gently, then with a big push, they rolled out of their eggs on to the grass. One by one, some with bits of shell sticking to their downy feathers, they came out. They blinked at the strange world all round them.

"Quack! Quack!" they called to each other, fluffing their wings.

The mother duck was very proud. She heaved herself off her nest and shook her feathers. One, two, three, four, five, six ducklings! She began to kick the broken shells out of the nest. She hated a mess. Then, she saw there was one egg left. It was a large one and needed longer to hatch.

"Oh dear," she said, and sat down again on the egg. "I'll have to go on sitting a bit longer."

An old duck waddled across the yard. "I see the ducklings have hatched," she said, sitting in the sun. "Fine, aren't they?" she watched them with a knowing eye. "Why are you still sitting?" she asked.

"There is one egg left," said the mother duck. "It's much bigger than the rest," and she got up to show the old duck.

"Forget it," said her friend, "it looks like a turkey to me. It's too big for any duck, so best leave it."

"Oh, I can't do that," said the mother duck. "I have sat so long already, a bit longer won't make any difference."

"I think you are silly," said the old duck. She waddled back to tell the others.

The mother duck did not have long to wait. With a louder "Quack" than the others, an ugly, grey scrap pushed its way out of the egg. It shook itself and looked around.

"What a funny little thing you are to be sure," said the mother. "Come and see your brothers and sisters." She shook her head. "I've never seen a duck like you before and that's a fact."

Quacking and pushing, the other ducklings crowded round their new brother.

"Oh, isn't he awful?" they said, pecking at him. "He's so ugly," said another, and they all laughed.

Soon the poor little duckling was hiding to keep away from their sharp beaks and teasing. "Come along now," said their mother, "no more fighting. You have got to learn to swim in the pond." And she pushed them all into the cool water. They all followed, the little grey one last of all. The mother duck swam out into the middle. The ducklings were soon splashing around her.

"It's lovely," they said, diving in and out and having a good time. The little grey one was a good swimmer, but he did not dare join in the games.

"Oh well, he's no turkey," said the mother, "he swims too well. But he's a very funny duck!"

At last it was time to go in. Time to meet the oldest duck in the farmyard. When she saw the little grey duck she shook her head. "Get him out of here," she said, "*that's* no duck! Send him away before he does harm." She flew at him, pecking his neck.

"Oh, leave him alone," said the mother, "he's doing no harm."

Soon, all the ducks and chickens began to tease the little duck. He was pecked here and squawked at there. His life was a misery. The old farm cat hissed at him and showed his claws. At last, he had had enough. He flew away over the hedge into the fields. Soon he came to the marshes where the wild ducks lived. Tired out, he crept among the rushes and lay down to sleep.

Next day the wild ducks found him. "Who are you?" they asked. "You are ugly! Go away, we don't want you here!" The little duck was very scared. "Please let me stay with you," he begged, "just for a little while."

They flew high into the sky and he watched them. How he wished he could be with them soaring up there in the clouds. Suddenly, there was a loud bang. First one, then another, and another, and two of the ducks dropped to the rushes. Men were calling and dogs barked, so the little duck hid himself deep in the weeds. A large dog ran into the rushes but stopped when he saw the duck. "Oh dear, even the dog is afraid of me," thought the little duck. "I must be the ugliest duck in the whole world."

That night, when all was quiet and the men and dogs had gone, the little duck crept out. The ducks had gone, too, and he was alone. He ran away as fast as his little legs would carry him.

At last he came to an old house and crawled in through a broken window. In the house lived an old woman with her cat and pet hen. She loved to stroke Puss's soft fur, and listen while she purred and arched her neck. The little hen laid big brown eggs and her mistress loved her very much.

You can imagine their surprise when they saw the duckling in the kitchen! "Oh what luck," said the old woman, "now I can have duck's eggs for my tea."

But the little duckling couldn't lay eggs. Soon the old woman scolded him. Then the cat clawed at him and the hen pecked him. No one wanted him. He remembered the marshes and the lake and wanted to go back. So, when the old woman opened the door, he ran away as far as his stumpy legs would carry him. He was so ugly, he had no friends, but he felt safe by the lake.

Autumn came. The leaves on the trees turned russet and fell. The air was cold and crisp, the hedgerows patterned with cobwebs. The duckling shivered. It would soon be winter.

One night, he looked up and saw a huge flock of white birds high in the sky. He had never seen anything so beautiful. Oh, their long necks! Oh, their strange cries: how he wished he could join them. But they were soon gone. He dreamed of them in the cold winter nights. He hoped so much to see them again.

It was a very cold winter. Snow sparkled on the ground and the lake froze. The duckling searched all round for food, but there was none. He was hungry and shivered in the weeds. The sun shining on the ice

was pretty and bright, like a mirror, but he could not swim. Soon he could not move, he was stuck fast in the ice. Then a kindly farmer took pity on him, and took him home to his family.

Once in the warm house, the little duckling felt better and flapped his wings. The farmer's children gave him some bread and milk. They wanted to play with him. But he was afraid of them and their noise. He flew up in the air, knocking over a jug of milk! It spread in a great white lake all over the floor. The farmer's wife was very cross and waved her arms. He flew higher and higher, then, tiring, came down, landing in a tub of butter! She clapped her hands and he scrambled out, all sticky, and fell into the flour bin. Everyone shouted at him. He was very frightened and flew out of the door as fast as he could.

At last, the long winter ended and the little duckling, by the lakeside, felt the first warmth of spring. The ice melted, the land grew green and everything felt alive. He shook himself and thought of the beautiful birds he had seen flying over. Would he ever see them again?

One day he flew high over the marshes and fields until he came to a large house. The garden was gay with flowers, and near the house was a large lake. But what was this? Swimming across the lake, pure and white, were some swans. The little duckling knew he must go to them.

"I must go and see them," he said to himself. "What does it matter if they peck me? It is better to die with such birds than live all alone. No one wants me. No one likes me. And I don't want to live alone for another winter."

So he swam across the lake, towards the swans in the distance. When they saw him, they paused. He stopped. "Kill me," he said, bowing his head. He waited. Nothing happened. Then the birds crowded round him. He looked down at the lake. Then he had a wonderful surprise! He could see, reflected in the water, *four* white birds! He looked again.

"Where have you come from?" the swans asked. "Where have you been hiding?'' And they laughed and flapped their wings.

He bowed his head and saw in the water a beautiful white bird do the same. He turned this way and that. So did the bird. Then he knew. It was him! He could see himself in the water. He was not ugly at all. He was a *swan*!

The other swans swam round him, stroking him with their beaks. "You are one of us," they said. "Welcome to the lake."

Just then, some children came to feed the swans.

"Look," they cried, "there is a new swan! Isn't he beautiful? He is the most beautiful swan we have ever seen!"

They threw some bread for him, and he was very happy. He thought he would burst with joy. All his dreams had come true. At last he had found the swans, and no one would ever call him ugly again. He was a pure white swan. A very fine swan indeed.

It's Perfectly True

"It is a shocking story," said the Hen, puffing out her feathers. "*The* most shocking story I have heard. All I can say," she went on, looking round, "all I can say, it is a good thing we roost together. I could not bear to sleep alone tonight. Not after this."

And, with everyone listening, all agog, she told her story again and again, until even the Rooster dropped his comb in horror.

It all happened in a hen house at the other end of town. The sun went down. It was evening. The hens flew up to their perch. One of them, a white-feathered bird, with short legs, who laid her eggs when she should and was no bother, settled on her perch. She was most respectable in every way. She preened herself on her perch, and plumed her feathers with her beak. A tiny white feather fell off and fluttered slowly to the ground.

"Let it go," she said without a thought. "The more I plume my feathers, the more they will grow."

Oh dear, she only meant it as a joke. Then she fell asleep. But her neighbour was awake, wide-awake, and she had heard what the little white hen said. She could not resist telling her neighbour.

"Did you hear? Well, I won't tell tales. But there is a hen—no, I won't say who it is—well she is going to pluck all her feathers, just to make herself beautiful."

Just above the hen house lived a family of owls. Of course, they were wide-awake during the night, and they had sharp ears. They heard every word the hens said.

"Don't take any notice," said Mother Owl. "If one hen wants to pluck all her feathers in front of the Rooster, well—" and she stopped.

"Don't say another word," said Father Owl. "We don't want the little ones to hear." Then he stretched himself. "I must go and tell our neighbours," and away he flew into the darkness of the night.

"Tu-whit, tu-whoo!" he hooted over the pigeon house. "Have you heard the news? There is a hen who has plucked out all her feathers, yes, *all* of them, just to please the Rooster. She must be freezing to death!"

"Where, where?" asked the pigeons, who were all ears at the story.

"In the yard over there. I saw it, with my own eyes! Not a pretty sight, but it's perfectly true!"

Away flew the pigeons, eager to tell the story in the hen yard below.

"Trrue, trrue," they cooed. "Listen, everyone. There's a hen, or maybe two hens, who have plucked out all their feathers. *All* of them, just to be different. They want to attract the Rooster, of course. It was an awful thing to do. And they are both dead of cold already."

All this noise woke the Rooster who always seemed to sleep with one ear open. "Cock-a-doodle-do!" he cried. "Wake up everybody. Three hens have died for love of a Rooster. They plucked out all their feathers. Tell everyone!"

"We'll tell, we'll tell," squeaked the bats. They hung upside down and heard everything that went on.

So the story went on and on. At last it came back to the hen-house where the little white hen was asleep.

"Five hens, five lovely hens are all dead because of vanity!" The

story went on. All the hens were listening now. "Five hens, are dead! They plucked out all their feathers, every one of them to please the Rooster. Then they pecked each other. Now they all are dead. What a shame and disgrace for everyone!"

"Whatever will their families think?" said the little white hen who was the cause of all the trouble. She did not recognize her own story, she was a respectable hen! She preened herself and said in a haughty voice, "I despise such silly creatures! Such tales should be known to stop others being so bad! I will make sure the papers hear of this. A tale like this must be told to everyone. No one shall be spared." And she puffed out her fine white feathers and felt important. The idea, indeed!

So the story was printed in the papers and everyone knew of the five hens. It's perfectly true. One small, white feather, carelessly dropped, without a thought, can easily become five hens.

The Tinderbox

The day was fine, and the Soldier sang as he came marching along the highway. Left! Right! Left! Right! His boots clanged and stomped on the hard road, and his feet kept pace with his song. His knapsack hung on his back, and his sword was at his side, but he was happy, for he was returning from the wars.

An old, bent Witch was coming along the road. She was very ugly, and her lower lip was full, and hung down close to her chest.

"Good evening, Soldier," she said. "That's a fine sword and knapsack you are wearing. You are a fine sight! You should have as much money as you could wish!"

"Thank you, Witch," said the Soldier. "I'm happy enough."

"Do you see that large tree?" asked the Witch, pointing her finger. "It is quite hollow inside. Go on, climb up to the top and you will see a large hole. Get down into the tree. But tie this rope round your waist, and I can pull you up when I hear you call."

"But what shall I do in the tree?" asked the Soldier. He wanted to get on home, but did not want to anger the Witch.

"Get the money," said the Witch. "As soon as you get to the bottom, you will find yourself in a large passage. It will be light, for more than a hundred lights burn there all day. You will see three doors, but you can open them. The keys are in the locks. Open the first door. Go down the staircase, and in the cave at the bottom there is a large chest. A dog is sitting on it with eyes as large as saucers. Don't mind him. I will give you my apron which you must spread on the floor. Then seize the dog and set him on it. He won't move. You can open the chest and take out as much money as you can carry. It is all copper."

The Soldier scratched his head. It all sounded very odd.

"Listen to me," said the Witch. "If you want silver, go into the next room. The dog there has eyes as big as mill-wheels, but don't mind him. Set him down on my apron and take what you want from the

chest. But, if you would rather have gold coins, go into the third room. The dog guarding that chest has eyes as large as a Round Tower. Pay no heed to him, just set him down on my apron and take what you want from the chest.''

"Not a bad idea, at that,'' said the Soldier. "But how much money do you want, old woman? You'll be wanting your share, I expect?''

"Of course, I do,'' said the Witch. "But I don't want money. Just bring me the old tinderbox you will find. My grandmother left it by mistake, the last time she was down there.''

"All right then,'' said the Soldier, "tie the rope round my waist, and I'll fill my pockets. And bring your tinderbox for you.''

"Here you are,'' said the Witch, and she tied the rope round the Soldier. "Take this apron.''

So the Soldier climbed up into the tree, let himself slowly down the hollow inside, and found himself in the wide passage of which the Witch had spoken. Gingerly, he opened the first door and went down the steps. There, just as she had said, was a dog with eyes as large as saucers. Quickly, the Soldier put down the apron, put the dog on it, and opened the chest. He soon filled his pockets. It was all very easy.

He went into the next room and, once more, just as the Witch had promised, there was a chest with a dog with eyes as large as mill-wheels. He laid down the apron again and before long, his clothes were weighed down with silver coins. He had never seen so many.

Now, for the third room. Even the Soldier was surprised to see this dog with its eyes as large as Round Towers, but he bravely laid down the apron as before and the dog was no trouble. Hastily, he grabbed all the gold coins he could find, stuffing them in his knapsack and even his boots. He had never seen so much gold in his life! With this wealth he could buy the whole town of Copenhagen, all the tin soldiers, sweets and rocking horses for the children. He was rich indeed. He put the dog back again, shut the door and called out to the Witch.

"Hey! I'm ready, pull me up again!''

"Have you got the tinderbox?'' she shouted to him.

"Oh, I forgot all about it!'' said the Soldier. "I'll go back for it.''

At last the Witch helped him out of the tree and he was standing beside her in the road. He was dropping gold coins from his pockets and boots, but he had plenty.

"What do you want with the tinderbox?'' he asked, "why don't you want a share of the gold?''

"That's my business," snapped the Witch. "You have your gold. Give me my tinderbox."

"We'll see about that," said the Soldier. "Not so fast! Tell me what you want to do with it, or I'll cut off your head."

"No! Give it to me!" screamed the Witch.

She made a grab for the box but the Soldier was too quick for her, and cut off her head! He put all the loose gold in the Witch's apron, slung it over his shoulder with his knapsack and picked up the tinderbox. Still singing, he went into the town.

It was the finest town he had seen in a long while. He went to the best inn, ordered the best food and wine and enjoyed himself. The servant did think though that his boots were very old for so rich a man.

Next day, all was changed. The Soldier went out and bought fine new clothes, and it was as though he had become a lord. He soon learned all about the town and the King who had a beautiful daughter. He wanted to meet her!

"How can I meet the Princess?" he asked.

"She is never seen at all," he was told. "She lives in a great copper palace surrounded by walls and towers. No one but the King may visit her. It has been foretold she will marry a common soldier and the King would not like that at all."

The Soldier thought how much he would like to meet her. But there was no sense in day dreaming. He lived a merry life, full of pleasure, but he never refused any beggars who asked his help. He spent freely and soon all his money was gone. There was not a single coin in his pockets! One day, he had to leave his lovely house, and live in a small attic. None of his friends would come to see him any more.

After a time one dark night, the Soldier had not even a match to light his one candle. Then he remembered the tinderbox, and he struck the flintstone. No sooner had he struck a spark, than the door burst open, and the dog with eyes as large as saucers sat before him and asked for his commands.

"Do you mean it?" asked the Soldier. "This is a fine tinderbox!" And he patted the dog. "Get me some money for a start," he said. In a few minutes the dog returned with a large bag of copper.

Then the Soldier understood the value of the tinderbox. If he struck it once, the dog from the copper chest would appear, so, if he struck it twice, the silver dog would come, and so on! And so it proved.

A rich man once more, the Soldier moved back to his fine rooms, and

all his friends came to see him. He thought again of the Princess and how much he wanted to see her.

That night he struck the tinderbox once more and, when the dog with eyes as large as saucers came, he said he would like to see the Princess. Before he could count ten, the dog was back, this time with the Princess on his back. She was more beautiful than the soldier could have dreamed. He kissed her and the dog ran back with her to the palace.

Next morning the Princess told the King she had had a strange dream. She had been riding on a dog, a huge dog, and she had met a soldier who had kissed her!

"A strange dream, indeed," said the King, and he insisted that a guard wait by the Princess' bedside.

But the Soldier was overcome with longing to see the Princess one more time, and he struck the tinderbox. The dog ran off to fetch her, and he was very quick. But not quick enough. The guard saw him and he followed, making a large cross on the door of the Soldier's house. Luckily, the dog noticed and put crosses on every house in town!

Early next morning the King and his men came to find the house but, as every house had a cross, their search was in vain.

The Queen had a clever plan. She made a little bag which she filled with buckwheat grains and tied it round her daughter's neck. She cut a little hole in the bag so the grains would fall wherever the Princess went.

In the night, the Soldier sent again for the Princess, for he truly loved her and wanted to marry her. The dog did not see the tiny grains of wheat falling on the ground, leaving a little trail to the Soldier's house. So, next morning, very early, the King and his men came to the house, and arrested the poor Soldier and took him to prison.

It was dark and cold in his cell, and the Soldier was very sad. "Tomorrow you will be hanged," said the jailer, "and serve you right too, if you ask me."

The Soldier racked his brains. Then he remembered the tinderbox which was still in his rooms.

Next morning the Soldier could hear the people hurrying to the market square, for they wanted to watch his execution. His cell was below the square, and he saw the legs of an apprentice running past.

"Wait!" he called, "would you like to earn a gold crown?"

The boy stopped. That was a fortune!

"If you go to my rooms and fetch me my tinderbox, I will give you a gold crown," said the Soldier. "But, *hurry*!"

The lad ran off and soon came back with the tinderbox.

The Soldier was taken out into the market place. A great crowd, with the King and Queen, had gathered to watch. As he stood there, with the hangman waiting, he spoke to the crowd.

"A boon," he craved. "One last request!"

"Be quick about it," growled the crowd.

"Let me smoke my last pipe," begged the Soldier.

The King granted his request and the Soldier took out the tinderbox. He rubbed it once, twice, three times. And, in a trice, the three dogs stood before him, asking for his orders.

"Save me," cried the Soldier. "Don't let them hang me!" So the dogs fell upon the judges and the council, tossing them into the air. There was shouting and confusion.

"Stop this!" shouted the King. But the dogs seized him as well!

The crowd, seeing this awful happening cried out to the Soldier that he could be their king and the Princess their queen, if he would call off his dogs.

So the poor Soldier made the story come true, and married the beautiful Princess. They lived happily in their castle and the three dogs always sat at the table, their eyes watching everyone in the room.

The Little Fir Tree

Far, far away in a deep, dark forest, there once grew a little fir tree. There were many fir trees in the forest, some tall and fine, others stumpy and feathery.

"Oh, how I wish I were tall!" sighed the little fir tree. He looked longingly at the bigger trees all around him and wished he could grow quickly. He did not want to wait.

The little fir tree was so filled with longing to be tall, he did not hear the murmur of the bees in summer, nor the song of the birds. He did not even hear the laughter of the children who came to play in the woods. They would sit under the trees to eat the wild strawberries they had gathered and look at the little fir tree.

"What a sweet little tree he is," they would exclaim and touch his branches, pretending to tickle him. The little tree would stand stiff and cross. They would not tease him if he were big and strong!

Year by year he grew, but he still longed to be able to stretch his branches wider and still wider. He wanted the birds to nest in his greenery, and to reach up and touch the blue sky above him. "I hate being small!" he would complain, and the older trees would smile and nod in the breeze.

When winter came, the ground was soon covered with a thick white mantle of snow and the trees looked very beautiful standing above it. They shook their branches and the snow fell silently on to the earth. There was a glistening, like silver when the ice and frost touched the trees. It was very quiet.

"Don't do that!" the little tree called to a hare who jumped over him. When two more winters had passed, the little tree had grown so much the hare had to run round him.

Time passed, and still the little tree was discontented. In autumn, the forest was busy with the sound of men's voices for they had come to cut down the big trees, and plant new ones. The little tree shivered a little when he heard the sharp tap and crack of the axes among the trees, and winced when he heard the tearing and crashing as a big tree fell. There was no sound like it. When one fell, the birds were silent and, for a while, there was a stillness in the woods. Then it began again, crack, tap, tap and soon another giant would shake itself as if reluctant to tumble, and crash to the ground. The men cut off the big branches, and the great trunks would lie bare in the dirt. The horses with their carts would come and the wood was loaded up and taken away. Where do they go? What happens to them? The little tree wondered, but no one told him. The swallows came back in the spring and the woods echoed to the sound of birdsong.

"What, still here?" they would tease the little fir tree, and he would try and ignore them. But he did so want to know what happened to the big trees.

"Where do the trees go?" he asked. "Have you seen them again?"

"We don't know," said the swallows, "we never see them. Be happy here in the forest." And they swooped and rose, laughing at him and his misery.

One day a wise old stork nodded her head. "I know where they go," she said. "Once, when I was young, I flew many miles, far away over the land of Egypt. I saw the tall masts of the big ships on the blue waters. They are the trees from the forest."

"If only I could be a mast and sail the seas!" thought the little fir tree, "but I am so small. I am too small for anything." And he sulked.

"But what is the sea? What is it like? Tell me all about it."

"It would take a lifetime," said the stork. "Be glad you are still in the green forest. The sea can be rough, and sometimes the great masts crack and break. Enjoy the summer while you can. You'll be big soon enough. Then you will wish you were still small." And she flew away to perch on the top of one of the highest trees. She looked down at the little fir tree, shaking in rage, and shook her head.

The dews came and the nights turned cold. All too soon it was winter again.

"Soon be Christmas," said the woodcutters when they came back to the forest. They liked their work, choosing the best trees for the children to enjoy. All that day they cut down one after another of the smaller trees in the forest. Soon, rows of them were carefully stacked at the edge of the clearing, waiting for the horse and cart to pick them up.

"Where do the little trees go?" The little tree still wanted to know. They could not be masts for tall ships, so what did they do with them?

"Do you know?" he asked the sparrows twittering in the branches.

"We can tell you," they told him. "We have seen them! In the city, which is full of houses, we have peeked in at the windows. We have seen the trees! They stand in the best place in the room and everyone looks at them! You cannot imagine it." And they flew up into the air.

"Wait!" The little fir tree wanted to know more. "Tell me more," he begged and they came back.

"Well, they are so beautiful! You cannot think how lovely they look with bells, and lights, and presents and tinsel! If you see them in a room, with the firelight glowing, it makes the bells ring, and the stardust glisten! Some have hundreds of tiny candles which dance in the firelight. Others have little packets of sweets hidden in the branches. You have never seen such a marvellous thing."

"And then?" asked the little fir tree, "what happens then?"

"Oh, we don't know," said the sparrows. "We only know they look so beautiful, decorated and shining. People come and stare at them."

The little fir tree grew excited. "I wonder if I shall be decorated one day," he said. "Will people come to see me?" He thought and thought about it. "I think I'd like that best of all. I don't want to grow big and tall for a ship's mast after all. I'd rather be decorated for a house in the city."

"Your time will come soon enough," the older trees told him. But the little fir tree cried when the carts pulled away with the trees piled in them. If only I were there, he thought.

One day he was the right size. And the woodcutters, arriving for the Christmas cutting, looked at him and agreed he was ready. He was the first to be cut down. The sharp tap of the axe hurt him and he fell to the ground feeling sore and shaken. Suddenly, he felt a fear at leaving the forest and his friends. But it was too late. All too soon, he was lying with lots of other trees in the back of the cart being jolted and bounced all the way to town.

In the city a man took out the trees one by one and shook them and looked at them. "This is just right," he said, "should make a good price." And he put the little fir tree against the wall so that anyone passing by would see him.

"This one will be fine for me," said a man's voice, and the little fir tree felt himself being lifted up by two men in smart red livery, and carried through the darkening streets until they came to a big house. The little tree felt glad. Soon he would be beautiful. He knew it.

Next day the little fir tree was placed in a huge tub filled with sand which tickled his trunk and he wanted to sneeze. He was dragged across the room into a corner by the window. He looked round. The room was large, with big, heavy chairs and tables and pictures on the walls. A little grey rocking horse nodded his head as if to welcome the little fir tree.

"What will happen next?" he wondered. He soon found out.

A tall man came into the room carrying a big box, then a lady came with scissors and string and two children followed.

"Just watch, children," said the lady, "don't get in the way. There is a lot to do." And the children sat on the floor and watched.

First, the man hung little, brightly-coloured baskets made of paper on the branches, each one filled with sweets. The little tree felt strange, and the branches bounced a little. Rosy, red apples were tied on, very carefully, with clusters of nuts nearby. Shadows from the fire made them look as if they were growing. "I'm a fruit tree!" the little fir tree laughed to himself.

Here and there little, odd-shaped parcels were tied. More and more things were threaded through the branches, until at last, came the moment the little fir tree had been waiting for: the candles were attached. One by one, in their holders, they were tied on.

"Please light them, just for a minute," begged the children. And the man took a taper from the fire and lit the tiny lights. The children clapped their hands in delight. The little fir tree glowed with pride. This was what he had longed for in the cold forest.

Later the lady came back with a ladder. She climbed to the top rung and, leaning over, fixed a large silver star at the very top of the tree.

"Now we are ready for Christmas!" she said.

The little fir tree wondered if the sparrows had seen him and would tell his friends in the forest how fine he looked. Would he always be there for all to admire? After a while, his branches began to ache. They were not used to such weights on them. His bark was tingling from the

sand, but he could do nothing. He tried to shake himself but felt a stinging as one of the candles dropped hot wax on him.

"Oh dear," said the lady, "we must be careful." And she blew out all the candles.

Next day was Christmas Day and all the candles were lit once more. The little fir tree stood very still and straight. This was his big moment. He was shining in all his glory, and would always remember this time. Soon the candles burnt low, and were put out. The children gathered round, and one by one, the parcels were ripped from his branches.

There were delighted cries as the parcels were opened, and the tree was forgotten. Some of his fine greenery was lying on the floor and the little needles fell in a cloud.

The children sat round the fire while their mother told them stories. The little fir tree listened until it was time for bed. What a day it had been! He felt very tired but very happy.

Very early next day before anyone else was up, two servants came into the room and woke the little fir tree. "They are going to dress me all over again," he thought. How wrong he was. How horribly wrong. For they had come to take him away. Quickly, they pulled him from the tub scattering sand on the floor, and took him up to the attic where he was thrown into an untidy room full of old, unwanted things. There was a doll with one arm, a toy horse with three legs, some broken chairs and an old horsehair sofa that smelt fusty. How horrid it is, thought the little fir tree. He did not like it at all. Everyone had forgotten him now.

46

Time passed and no one bothered about the little tree. A man came and pushed some more boxes into the room, but did not look at the tree. "It is winter," the little tree thought, "maybe it is too hard to plant me in the garden. I shall have to wait here until the spring comes and the ground is soft once more. Then I can go on growing."

Some mice began scampering round him, but he did not like them at all. Birds were much nicer he thought. The mice jumped all over him. "Where do you come from?" they asked. "Isn't it lovely here?" But he did not answer. How could he tell them of the green, green forest and the sun and the smell of pine?

At last spring came again and the sun shone through the dusty windows. "Now I shall be planted in the garden," thought the little fir tree.

One morning he was carried downstairs and taken out to the garden. The air was clean and fresh, and he was happy. It was a lovely day and the children were in the garden. They came when they saw the tree.

"There's the star!" they cried and took it off. They began jumping on the tree, snapping his branches. "Poor old tree, poor old tree," they chanted, "old brown tree!" And they left him on the ground. He wished he had been left in the attic.

At last, one of the gardeners came. He chopped the little fir tree into small pieces, and piled them in a great pile. Then, while the children watched, he took a match and lit the wood. It was very dry and it crackled and jumped! The little fir tree sighed deeply, and each sigh was like the sound of a shot.

The little fir tree thought of the cool, green forest, how it shone in the winter's snow or was bright when the rain washed the dust from the branches. All too soon, he was a heap of ashes.